SASHA visits BALI

Illustrated by Alpana Ahuja
Written by Shamini Flint

Book One: Sasha in Asia

Sasha is in Bali!

She walks down the street and stops at a shop.

"Look, Mamma! Look at the cats!"

"Those cats are carved from wood, Sasha."

Sasha is amazed at the unusual toys in the shop.

She spots a butterfly kite, carved wooden fish and bamboo wind chimes.

Can you see them too?

Mamma and Sasha are at the beach.

Sasha is flying a wonderful kite.

It is shaped like a sailing ship.

The wind is taking it higher and higher!

Sasha wriggles her toes in the golden sand.

She *is* enjoying her holiday.

The next day Mamma and Sasha
visit a paddy field.

Sasha points at the farmers.

"What are they doing, Mamma?"

"They are planting new seedlings
on the terraces, Sasha."

"What do we get from paddy fields, Mamma?"

"Delicious rice, Sasha!"

The next stop for Sasha and Mamma is the Monkey Forest in Ubud.

"Sasha, look at all the monkeys!"

Sasha and Mamma have brought bananas for the monkeys.

"Mamma, I can see a baby monkey!"

Can you spot the baby monkey?

Sasha loves dressing up!

Mamma has borrowed a beautiful costume
for Sasha.

Sasha is pretending to be a Balinese dancer.

The people of Bali have many unique and
interesting dances.

Some dancers are children just like Sasha!

That evening, Mamma and Sasha watch the sunset over the sea.

The sky looks as if it is on fire
and the colours are reflected in the water.

Sasha and Mamma can see the
beautiful temple of Tanah Lot.

The temple is cut off from the mainland
when the tide is high.

In the morning, Sasha and Mamma visit the beach again.

A surfer is rushing to shore on the foaming waves.

Another surfer is carrying his surfboard under his arm.

Sasha has her hair braided with colourful beads.

It feels strange!

It makes a clickety-clackety sound when Sasha shakes her head from side to side.

Mamma and Sasha attend a *wayang kulit* performance.

It is a very unusual puppet show.

The puppets are used to cast shadows on a screen!

Sasha has her hand in the air.

She is trying to make a shadow on the screen too.

Mamma whispers, "Put your hand down, Sasha!"

Sasha is walking through a Balinese garden.

It is full of exquisite, tropical flowers.

Even the fierce-looking statue has flowers behind its ears!

Sasha is on her way home in an aeroplane.

She enjoyed every minute of her Bali holiday.

She looks out of the window at the airport below.

"Mamma, let's come back here soon!"

The "Sasha in Asia" Books

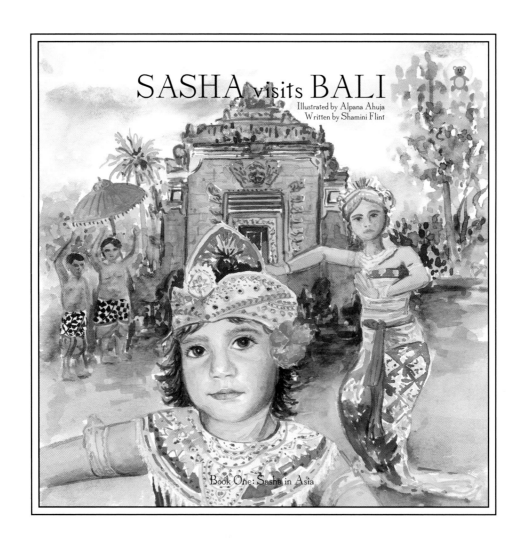

SASHA visits BALI

Illustrated by Alpana Ahuja
Written by Shamini Flint

Book One: Sasha in Asia

The "Sasha in Singapore" Books